Storyteller's Note

Birds are everywhere. Throughout the ages, poets, scholars, and common folk have been fascinated by the songs of birds. Sometimes their whistles, trills, and chirps have reminded people of words or sounds they know; those words or sounds are frequently used to describe the songs of many birds—and especially to help us identify birds in the wild.

For Rosalie Heacock and Estelle Busch, who know the birds' songs

—A. W.

In memory of my father, Henry Florczak

—R. F.

CAW-CAW-CAW—swaying on telephone wires, jaunty crows banter at dawn. Missy and Deni awaken to birdsong.

For breakfast Armando and Juan eat tortillas, eggs, and beans.
WHAT-CHEER, WHAT-CHEER, WHEAT-WHEAT-WHEAT—
saucy cardinals chatter just beyond their window.

Traffic lights change, taxis race down big city streets. Nearby there's a little park nestled among the skyscrapers. While Jordan and Elly play, gentle pigeons splash and make their cooing calls—COO-A-ROO, COO-A-ROO, COO-A-ROO.

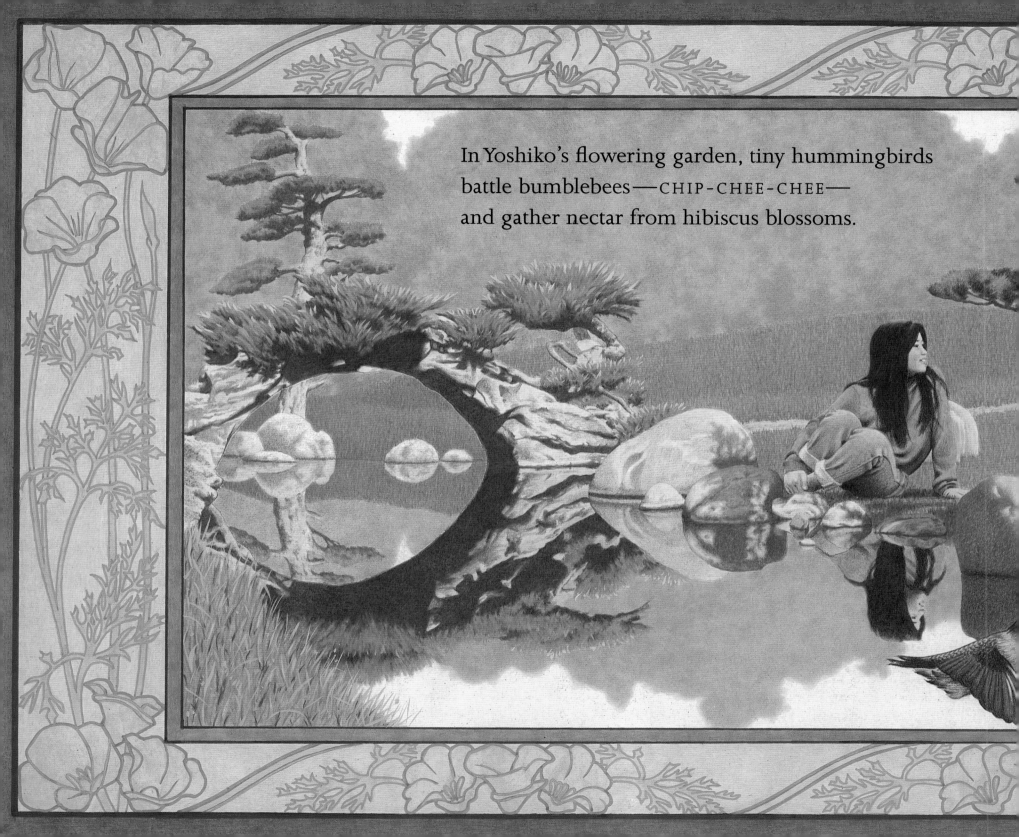

In Yoshiko's flowering garden, tiny hummingbirds battle bumblebees—CHIP-CHEE-CHEE—and gather nectar from hibiscus blossoms.

Over the hills, down in the valley, Roger and Don begin their morning chores. BOB-O-LINK, BOB-O-LINK, SPINK-SPANK-SPINK—chattering bobolinks search for tasty morsels in plowed fields. DEAR-ME, DEAR-ME, DEAR-ME—swift goldfinches swoop over cornstalks ripening in the sun.

For a secret lunch, Jason's neighborhood friends meet in their tree house hideaway. CHICK-A-DEE-DEE-DEE—friendly chickadees flutter down to eat walnuts from their hands.

Where can the Miller twins go when the sun burns through
their T-shirts and their hot feet ache in their laced-up sneakers?
Down to the cool, moss-banked pond, where—GAWK! GAWK!—
startled herons fly up from water reeds with salamanders
dangling from their beaks.

The day is long, there's plenty of time for adventure, so Ranto and Navara paddle down a winding river. RICKITY-CRICK-CRICK, RICKITY-CRICK-CRICK—crafty kingfishers dive for insects, tadpoles, and silvery minnows.

Up in the mountains on wildflower trails, the air is thin and the summer moon shines pale in a sunny sky. Jim and Lou stop to listen—KEEYER, KEEYER, KEEYER. Fearless hawks soar high above their heads as they search for prey.

Everyone is hungry on the Dalton Ranch. Down in the grassy meadow plump bobwhites gossip—BOB-WHITE, BOB-WHITE—as they bob for juicy berries. CHICKY-TUCKY-TUCK—musical tanagers sing while feeding their fledglings.

After a snack Bernard and Francis lie down for a nap, but who can rest in the noisy bayou? YUCCA-YUCCA-YUCCA— determined woodpeckers drum on dead tree limbs. PUMPERLUNK, PUMPERLUNK—suspicious bitterns fuss while hiding in cattails, and busy rails call—KEK-KEK-KEK—while spearing crawdads.

As afternoon shadows stretch like long fingers on the forest floor, Alex chases Andrew. TEACHER-TEACHER-TEACHER— bossy ovenbirds scold from low branches.

Now the sun is down and the day is done. WHIP-POOR-WILL, WHIP-POOR-WILL—the worried whippoorwill calls Dahlia and Oren home.

WHO? WHO? WHO? Snug in their cozy beds, Daniel and Bruce are searching for sleep. WHO? WHO? WHO?—a questioning owl hoots from a hollow in her tree. The day ends as it began, with birdsong.

Requests for permission to make
copies of any part of the work should be mailed to:
Permissions Department, Harcourt Brace & Company,
6277 Sea Harbor Drive, Orlando, Florida 32887-6777.

Library of Congress Cataloging-in-Publication Data
Wood, Audrey.
Birdsong/by Audrey Wood; illustrated by Robert Florczak.
p. cm.
Summary: Children across the land hear birdcalls native
to their areas as they go through their daily activities.
ISBN 0-15-200014-3
[1. Birdsongs—fiction.] I. Florczak, Robert, ill. II. Title.
PZ7.W846Bi   1997
[Fic]—dc20   95-45737

First edition
A C E F D B

───────────

The illustrations in this book were done in Tombow water-based
markers, gouache, colored pencil, and opaque ink on blueprint paper.
The display type was set in University Bold.
The text type was set in Joanna.
Color separations by Bright Arts, Ltd., Singapore
Printed and bound by Tien Wah Press, Singapore
This book was printed on totally chlorine-free Nymolla Matte Art paper.
Production supervision by Stanley Redfern and Ginger Boyer
Designed by Michael Farmer

The artist would like to thank the Los Angeles County Museum of Natural History,
the San Bernardino County Museum, the Los Angeles chapter of the Audubon Society,
and Anthony Mann for their assistance in his research.